Things were disappearing in our house— ev ry day. Like, a LOT!

The Scissors. The Car keys!
The TV Remote !!! ONE SOCK.
HOMEWORK that we
have actually DONE !!!....
OUR PARENTS THINK IT'S US!!!
PLEASE, IF YOU GET
This message,
HELP US!!

US

BALLOON

Message

Suddenly, we were sucked down a tube and into a most interesting laboratory.

"I am Dr. Zooper," said a fellow who looked very Zooperish. "The problems you mentioned in your note are caused by a race of pesky creatures called Mischievians." Dr. Zooper then pointed to a lively volume that stood open before us.

"All the questions that you have will be answered in this book."

And so we began.

The MISCHI

An encyclopedia of things that make mischief, make mayhem, make noise, and make you C R A Z Y !

EVIANS

Fig. Heebie Jeebies, see page we don't know yet

Compiled with illuminations by Dr. Maximilian Fortisque Robinson Zooper, MD, PhD, LOL, OMD, QED, & Golly Gee. Done while snapping his fingers in the air. Just kidding. Mayb

THE HOMEWORK EATER

Fig. 12 Yum Lern

Question:

Okay, Dr. Zooper, here's a biggie: *Sometimes* I know I've done my homework, but the next morning, I can't find it. *Sometimes* I get to school, and *then* I can't find it. *Sometimes* I get to school, and I turn it in, but then my *teacher* can't find it! *Sometimes*—

Answer:

I get your drift. Your homework was not eaten by your dog or your little brother or taken by aliens. Well, probably not any of the aliens *I've* studied, anyway. Your homework was stolen by a *Mischievian* called a Homework Eater.

Question:

Um . . . why does it eat homework?

Answer:

Oddly enough, Homework Eaters aren't trying to be mischievous. You see, every Homework Eater begins his life by being extremely dumb. But they love knowledge. They eat it up. Literally. The more they eat, the smarter they become.

Question:

How did Homework Eaters eat homework in olden times?

Answer:

I love that question! In the 1700s they were called Ye Olde Eaters of Homestead Studies.

Wisdom Munchers would, of course, eat the clay tablet assignments of ancient Babylonian boys and girls.

The Crunch Rock Swallow Smarts of cavemen times would eat homework that was actually chiseled in stone.

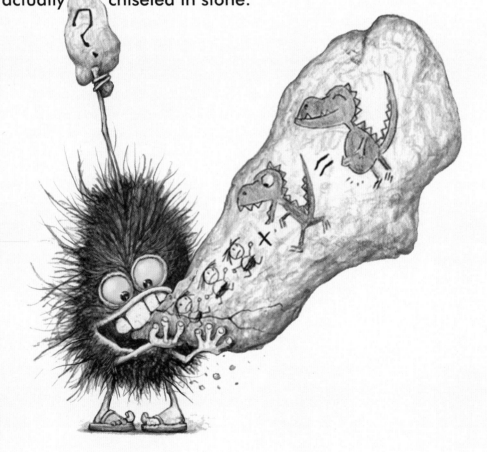

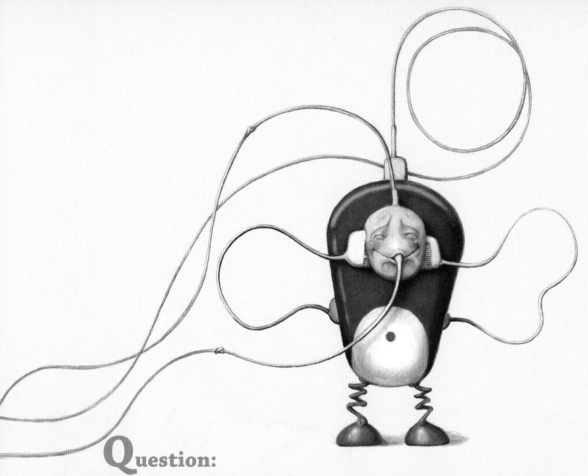

Question:

Can Homework Eaters steal homework from computers?

Answer:

Superb question! Yes! That is their favorite new source of knowledge. Some Homework Eaters have evolved into File Suckers, a completely new sub-species of Homework Eaters.

Question:

Is it possible Homework Eaters could someday eat my homework and so much other knowledge that they will become superadvanced, genius Mischievians who will rule our world?

Answer:

I think that happened last Tuesday.

THE FILE SUCKER

Fig. 2030 Brain Suk

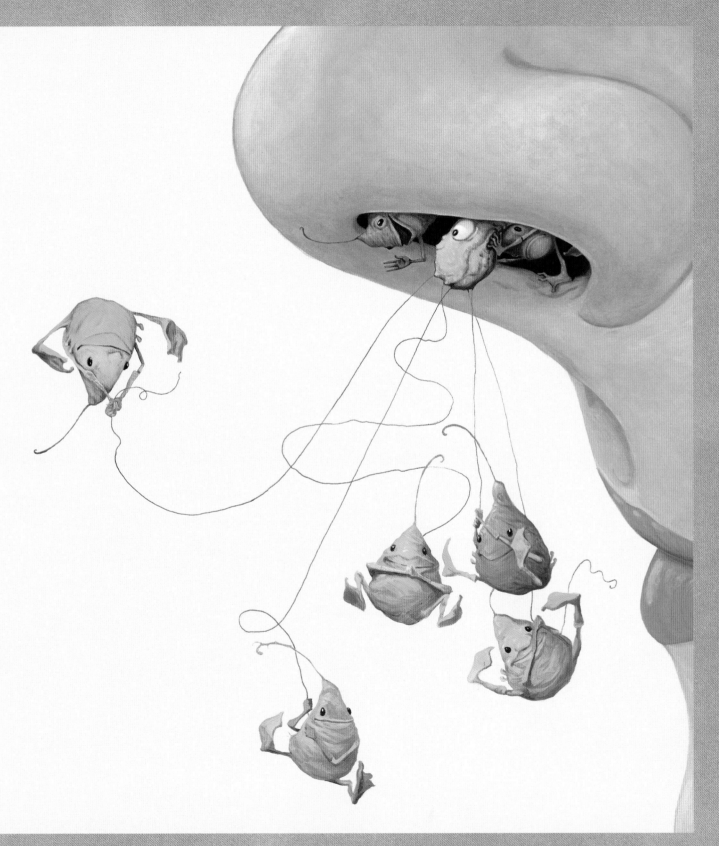

THE DANGLERS

Fig. 70 Gboog

Question:

Dr. Zooper, you know when you look in the mirror and see a booger dangling out of your nose and you know it's been there maybe all day and everybody has probably seen it? Did a Mischievian do that?

Answer:

Yes! This mischievous duty is performed by Danglers. A small group of Danglers live in your nose. Their only job is to lure the nervous Booger out of the nostril. (Boogers are notoriously shy.) Once out, Boogers discover that they love to see and be seen. When the Booger is visible, the Danglers return to their hideout in your nose. Never be embarrassed by a Booger that is dangling. A dangling Booger is a happy Booger.

Question:

Do I have to leave the Booger dangling?

Answer:

That's between you and your Booger.

Question:

Are Mischievians responsible for belly button lint?

Answer:

Yes! Lintbellians are among the most harmless of all Mischievians. They do not break things, spill things, hide things, or hurt things. They cause only minor embarrassment. I mean, let's face it. Who doesn't sort of like belly button lint? I mean, really.

Question:

So where do Lintbellians come from?

Answer:

Amazing question! Lintbellians are not actually produced by your belly or its button. They are made of *lint*.

Question:

And where does this lint come from?

Answer:

Mostly from socks. Have you ever noticed those little knobby balls that form on the heels of your socks? When a Sock Stalker[*] steals a sock, he picks off all the Lint Balls. The newly emancipated Lint Balls will then make the long journey to find the person whose socks they once clung to. They seek out the safest, warmest place they can find: that person's belly button. There, they transform into Lintbellians and live in happy solitude until discovered and their belly button home is cleaned out.

But don't feel sorry for the Lintbellians. As you may have noticed, they always come back.

[*]See Sock Stalkers

THE LINTBELLIAN   *Fig. 1171 Ooohbelly*

A MISTA BLISTA

Fig. 30 Toez

Question:

Where do blisters come from?

Answer:

Ah! That would be the work of a Mischievian called a Mista Blista.

Every shoe has several Mista Blistas living inside it. They usually hide in the toe area until you put on the shoe. They are rather smooshy, and usually give you no problem at all. However, when you've been wearing your shoes for a really long time, your feet can get extremely hot and sweaty.

Mista Blistas *love* hot, sweaty feet. They become so happy that they swell with joy. Once swollen, they rub up against your feet (which makes them even happier). The result? *They* are very happy and *you* get a blister.

Question:

But why do new shoes give you blisters after just a few minutes?

Answer:

Brilliant question! When you get a new pair of shoes, you also get a new troupe of Mista Blistas. These "newbies" are so proud to be on their first mission that they swell with joy *and* pride, causing immediate and painful blisters.

Question:

Okay, here's a question that could save my dad's sanity: Does a Mischievian have anything to do with missing TV remotes?

Answer:

Yes! Yes! Yes! Fiendish creatures called RemoteToters are responsible for lost or misplaced remotes of all kinds: televisions, stereos, gates, and garage doors.

RemoteToters are currently among the most feared of all Mischievians and have been known to cause not only fathers, but also entire families, to completely lose their minds.

They move with blinding speed and have many eyes that alert them to any possibility of being caught. They can also change colors to match whatever they are running across as they hide the remote in the most irritating place possible.

They are so mischievous, they have been known to move the remote several times during a mission, oftentimes returning it to a place they know everyone has already looked—usually under the couch cushion or, most irritatingly, the exact place it was last seen.

THE REMOTETOTER

Fig. 20 Totty

THE STICKER

Fig. 13 Stkr

Question:

Why do I sometimes get a thorn thingy stuck in my foot when I walk barefoot in the grass? I look around, but I never see where it came from.

Answer:

And you *never will*. In every yard, park, and field of grass, there is a tiny, stealthy army of Mischievians called Stickers, who make it their mission to stick you in the foot.

Question:

So when I pull out the thorn thingy, am I pulling out an actual Sticker?

Answer:

Sort of! In point of fact, it's the nose of a Sticker. Their special detachable schnozzolla can be shot like an arrow into the soft, vulnerable underside of any approaching foot.

Question:

But why?

Answer:

They're called Stickers. *It's their job. It's what they do!*

Question:

What can I do to keep away from Stickers?

Answer:

Wear shoes.

Question:

Sometimes I get something sticky on my fingers—like, *between* my fingers—and they keep sort of sticking together. And it won't wash off FOR A LONG TIME. Or all of a sudden there's a spot on one of my shoes that sticks to the floor, and I can feel it when I walk, and it makes this little sticky sound, and it really bugs me. Why does this happen?

Answer:

You've been struck by a Sticky. Historically, Stickys have been found in the stickiest places on Earth. The back shelf of the refrigerator. Underneath a car's cup holders. Around the cap of a ketchup bottle. And any place a baby has been.

Not much is known about Stickys, but scientists generally agree that babies (until they are three years of age) are the single stickiest things in the known universe. Bathe them all you want. Wipe them off a thousand times a day. Within seconds, the hands, feet, and faces of babies become amazingly sticky.

And what we still don't know is this: How does the chain of stickiness work? Does all stickiness, and therefore Stickys themselves, actually come from babies? Or do Stickys make babies so, well, sticky?

This much is certain: It can't all come from juice boxes.

THE STICKY

Fig. 5050 Stke

THE STINKER

Fig. 4 Peeyoo!!

Question:

Sometimes there's a bad smell in our house. My mom blames it on my shoes. She blames it on our dog. She blames it on our dad. Are any of these things making the stink?

Answer:

Yes and no. The various bad odors, smells, and aromas that occasionally befoul your home are almost always the work of the Stinkers.

Every Stinker has a suitably stationed trumpet from which to emit his stink, and a dial to control the level and flavor of stink.

Stinkers consume and store any bad smell they can find—rotten eggs, soured baby formula, dirty diapers, or anything nasty you might have stepped in. Their collection of stink is endless.

Question:

Okay, is that smell *outside* of our bathroom because of a Stinker?

Answer:

No, that's usually because of your dad.

Question:

How long have Stinkers been stinking?

Answer:

Scientific studies show that Stinkers are among the most ancient of Mischievians. They appear in cave paintings and on ancient Egyptian scrolls.

Stinkers love bad smells above all else. With their prominent proboscis (nose), they can detect a deliciously awful smell from thousands of miles away. They can smell great stinks of the past (spoiled yak milk from the lost city of Atlantis) or even stink of the future (rotten Twonk droppings from the planet Glumpt).

Louie the Stinkteenth

320 BC

WAY olde STINKER

Stinkiest toe in history
Sir Vilomont Yuckfoot

STINKERS OF YORE

Fig. 1001½ Pee Yoo Hoo

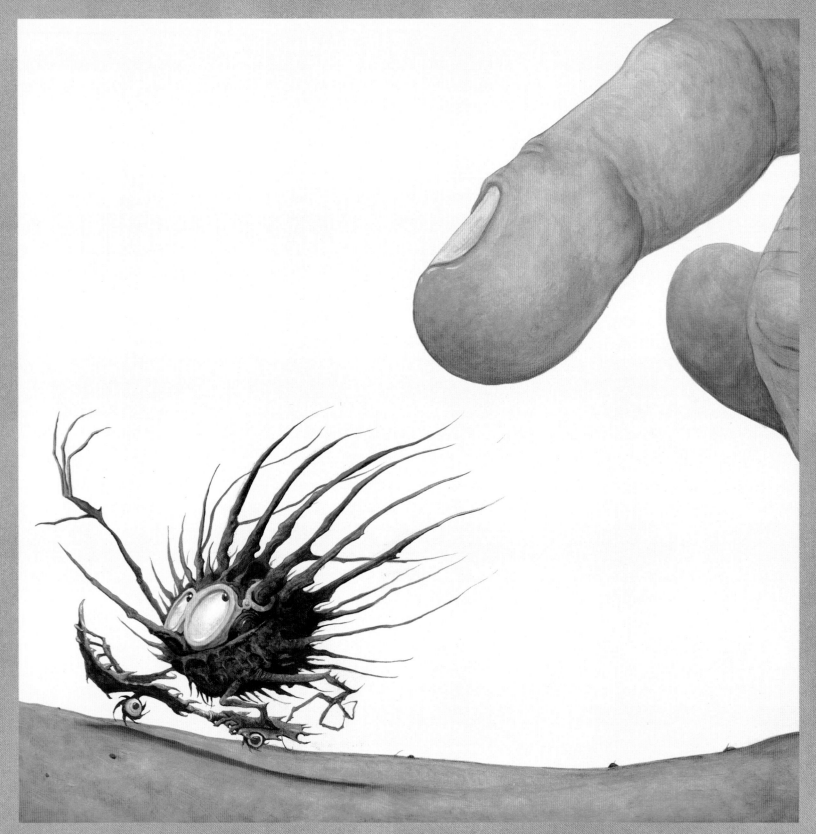

THE ITCHY

Fig. 007 Nay Nay Nay

Question:

All right, sometimes I get this itch on a part of my back that I can't *ever* reach. I twist. I turn. I streeeeeetch, but it's always just . . . out . . . OF . . . REACH! And it drives me *crazy*! Do Mischievians do that?

Answer:

Yes, indeedy! This bit of mischief is performed by an extremely tiny creature called the Itchy. Don't worry if his itch drives you insane. It's supposed to! That's how an Itchy knows he's doing his job.

Question:

When does an Itchy usually strike?

Answer:

Ah! He loves to strike at the worst possible time. When you're in front of class doing a report. Any time you have to wear nice clothes and sit still. (Nice clothes are naturally hot and itchy and fit too tight, so it's even harder to reach the Itchy.) Worst of all, they stage full-scale multiple itch attacks when you're trying to go to sleep. Remember, they are amazingly well equipped to evade any attempt to scratch them. They are small, swift, and always able to skate juuuuuuuust out of reach.

So relax. Go insane. The Itchy will think his job is done and go away.

Maybe.

Question:

Okay. I'm walking along. Everything's fine. Then—*BAM!* I hit my elbow. It sort of hurts and sort of feels funny. But not ha-ha funny. Just weird-I-can't-move-my-arm-for-a-minute-oh-oh-oh-that-kinda-hurts funny. What's up with that?

Answer:

You did not hit your funny bone. You have been attacked by a Funny Bones. And though you may find nothing funny about it, a Funny Bones thinks the entire mission is hilarious.

Question:

But it hurts. And that's bad, right?

Answer:

No, it's good. Funny Bones become so amused that they become completely helpless and must hide out until their laughter passes. Sometimes for up to two months. That's why your funny bone is hit only about six times a year.

THE FUNNY BONES

Fig. 66 Ha-Ha

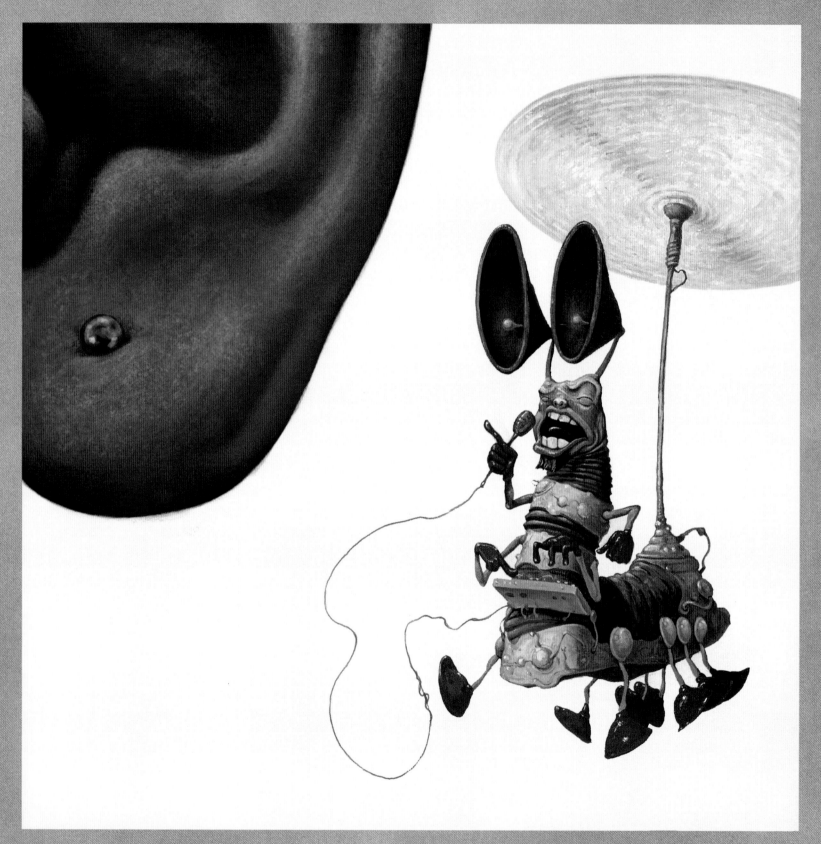

THE EARWORM

Fig. 0000 La La La

Question:

Why do I get songs I hate stuck in my head?

Answer:

Ahhhh. You've been attacked by the single most dreaded of ALL Mischievians: the Earworm!

Earworms learn every bad song that's ever been written. And they know all the songs that you reeeeeeally hate.

They sing them quietly in your ear, just before you wake up in the morning. Or make someone near you hum one. Or have one played on the TV or at the mall. Songs that are so awful and so irritating that just saying their titles will get them stuck in your head for hours, days, months. *Forever.* UNTIL YOU GO INSANE.

Question:

How can I keep from getting earwormed?

Answer:

Whatever you do, don't even *think* about what song you hate, because the Earworm will know and you will *get wormed*.

Question:

How do I get rid of a song if I get earwormed?

Answer:

There's only one antidote: get a glass of water, stand on one foot, and gargle the national anthem for ninety seconds. It works every time.

Question:

Sometimes when I'm really, *really* not supposed to laugh—like when it's something really, *really* serious—I start to laugh and I CANNOT STOP. Why?

Answer:

Ouch! That's a tough one. And one of the most embarrassing. The Giggler has an amazingly developed sense of when you should *not* laugh, then sends you into uncontrollable giggles until everyone thinks you are rude, stupid, insensitive, or insane! Weddings. Tests.   inners with grown-ups in nice restaurants—these are the playgrounds of the Gigglers. They have large and extremely ticklish feet, which they rub together till they generate a powerful amount of "funnergy." The Giggler then aims its giggle ray at an unsuspecting target. Usually you. Suddenly, you will feel an uncontrollable need to laugh. Anything even slightly humorous (a hiccup, someone snorting, a burp, or sometimes absolutely NOTHING AT ALL) will then unleash an attack of the giggles that will last until the funnergy is released and you are in trouble.

THE GIGGLER

Fig. 7,000 T Heehee

THE ENDROLLER

Fig. 13 Uh-Oh

Question:

Why does no one *ever* admit that they used *all* the toilet paper?

Answer:

That is sooo easy! Humans *never* use all the toilet paper. Humans are *very* thoughtful. It is the Endroller who unfurls toilet paper like there was no tomorrow! And why do you never ever find this wasted toilet paper? Because he unrolls it *into the toilet* for his friend who is even more annoying. . . . .

Question:

Who's the Endroller's friend?

Answer:

PERFECT QUESTION!!! The Clog-La-Dite! Clog-La-Dites are the fiendish little toilet dwellers whose sole purpose is to secretly *clog* the *toilet*! And you take the blame!

Question:

They live in the toilet? All the time?

Answer:

Yes.

Question:

That's pretty yucky.

Answer:

Yes, it is yucky. And it is not pretty.

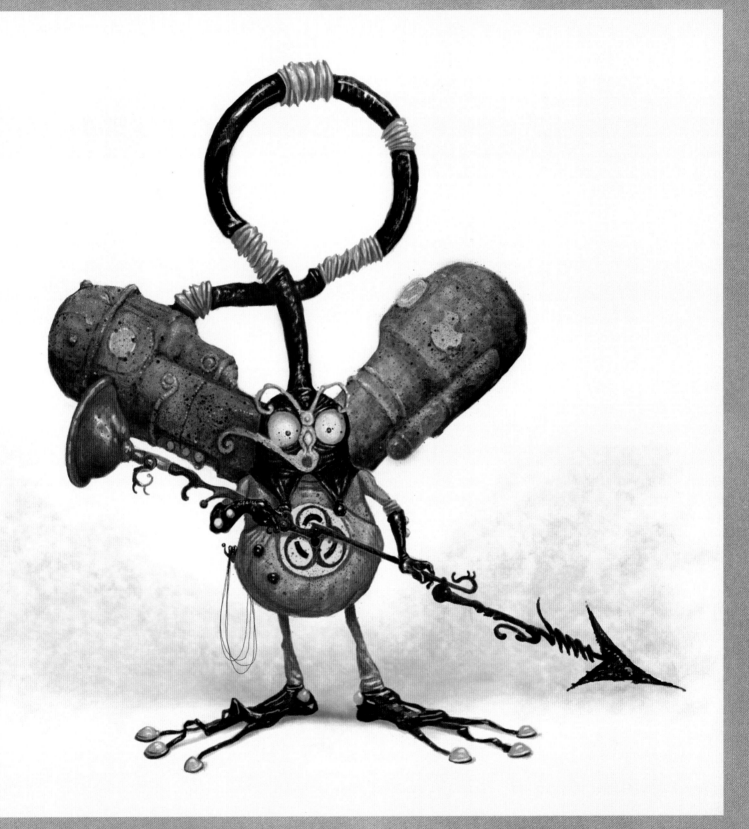

THE CLOG-LA-DITE

Fig. 1,000 Zillion Yuck

THE SOCK STALKER

Question:

Everybody in our house has, I dunno, at least six pairs of socks that are missing one sock!

Where does that sock go?

Answer:

Ooooooooh. A supremely good question. Since the invention of socks (which occurred on the lost continent of Atlantis), humans have been plagued by the Sock Stalkers. These smallish, hairy creatures insist on stealing ONE, and only ONE, of a pair of socks. The reasons for this are threefold. First, Sock Stalkers love socks more than anything. Second, Sock Stalkers can only count to ONE. Third (and most important), when they see more than one of a sock, it disturbs them so deeply that all their hair will immediately fall out. They hate to be seen naked, so they frantically gather up their fallen hair and wrap t emselves in *single* socks until no part of their bare skin can be seen.

Question:

Are they *really* shy?

Answer:

No! Just self-conscious. They are the only creatures alive who have eleven belly buttons.

Question:

But they can only count to one?!

Answer:

That's right! Having eleven belly buttons really freaks them out.

Question:

Yawning is so weird. What makes us yawn?

Answer:

Wow! You're the first person to *ever* ask! Well, believe it or not, being sleepy does not produce yawns. They are made by Yawn Mowers. Yawn Mowers are members of the Oddsoundians family of Mischievians. These are the Mischievians who cause humans to make odd and embarrassing sounds. Oddsoundians include the Burbbits, the Achoodlie-Doos, the Cough-E-Makers, the Snoreman Knights, and the most infamous and humiliating of all Mischievians, the Pootles.

Question:

Do Pootles . . . make you, umm . . . you know, like . . .

Answer:

Yes.

Question:

Um . . . what do they look like?

Answer:

Trust me. You don't want to know.

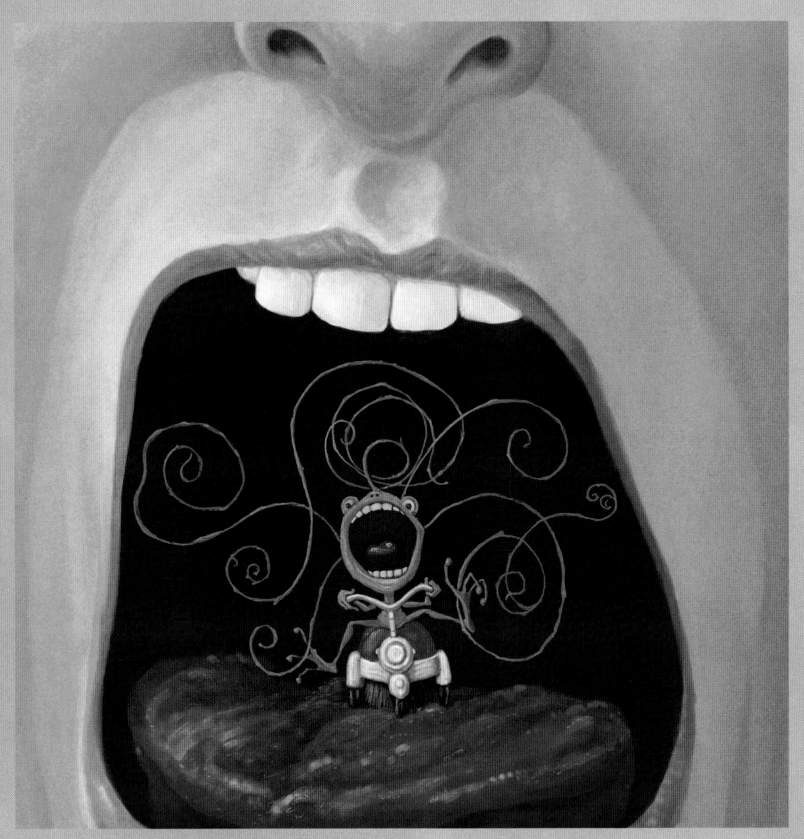

THE YAWN MOWER

Fig. 6 Yaaaoh

"Well, that's all the time we have for today's questions," concluded Dr. Zooper. Before we could say "but wait a sec" or "thank you" or "may we stay forever," we were zooped back up the chute.

However, the good doctor did give us a parting gift: our own Mischievians book! "Write down any Mischievians you discover. I will gladly include them in the Mischievians files!" he shouted as we vanished.

The books and robots waved good-bye and somehow I lost a shoe. But it was worth it.

"Wow! That was fun."

"LOOK!
There's a blank page!
I hope we find some
Mischievians!"

"You think there are any around?"

MISCHIEVIAN REPORT: TOP SECRET

MISCHIEVIAN NAME:

TYPE OF MISCHIEF:

HISTORY:

SIZE:

COLOR:

LEVEL OF MISCHIEF:

☐ MINOR   ☐ MUDDLING   ☐ WAY BAD

PLACE DRAWING OR PHOTO HERE ⬆

ANYTHING ELSE YOU'D LIKE TO ADD:

the

enD

?